Bitten Apple

CHRISTOPHER PEOPLES

This is a work of fiction. Names, characters, businesses, places, events, locales, and incidents are either the products of the author's imagination or used in a fictitious manner. Any resemblance to actual persons, living or dead, or actual events is purely coincidental.

CONTENTS

CHAPTER 1

It's the most beautifulist thing in this world, borrowing from the great Keith Murray. Holy matrimony, the day when people gather to witness the vowing of two people's love. Therefore, today, we are gathered to witness my best friend, John, vow his love to his queen, Apple. Before the ceremony began, the wedding planner sent John and me to a dressing room to keep him from running into the bride while the bride and her bridesmaids were taking pictures. I've never understood the bad luck of seeing the bride before the wedding, but it gives me a few last moments to spend with John before the wedding.

As soon as we got in the room, John started his nervous

rants. Man, what's up with this tie? I can't get this tied for shit.

I stood up, confused but understanding the situation, and walked over to John. Bruh, one question, how in the hell can you lead an army of grown men into war, but tying a tie frustrates you?

Man, shut up and bring yo ass over here and help me. Plus, leading men into war is not the same as being married, Chris.

How do you figure that? I've been married for years, trust me, being married is exactly like going to war.

Whatever Chris, you may have been married for a while, but you know nothing about leading men into war. War takes things from you that can never be replaced. Apple adds to me. She gives me things only love can provide.

Absolutely. I didn't mean to take away anything Apple provides to your sanity and happiness. Apple is an incredible woman. Ever since we've been in grade school, it's been obvious she would be your wife.

John stands, looking in the distance with a stupid grin on his face. Yeah, I guess so. I adore Apple. She's the best thing that ever happened to me. I hope I can make her feel the way she makes me feel.

Fuck that mushy shit, bruh; you got plenty of time to cry during the ceremony. Right now, just enjoy the experience. Soak everything in, take today slow, relax, breathe and let the moments come to you. Everything is beautiful. The venue is incredible, the flowers and fixtures are in place, the pastor is ready, all the groomsmen and bridesmaids are here and the car is ready to take us to the reception. The wedding planner is doing a tremendous job, and most importantly, Apple still wants to marry your dumb ass. Laughing and putting the final touches on his tie, I continue, so shut the fuck up, let me finish with this tie and let's get the hell out of this dressing room and get to our place for the ceremony.

You know what, you're right. Before I forget, I wanted to thank you for being here with me and standing as my best man. I couldn't have asked for a better friend to go through this with me.

Standing in the mirror for a last check of the whole suit, I ask, how you feeling bro? By the end of the day, you'll be a married man.

I feel great! Marrying Apple is a dream come true. Any advice from an old vet in the marriage game?

Laughing, yeah, don't do it!

A look of concern comes over John's face; what the fuck you mean, don't do it? Apple is the perfect woman; there's nothing I wouldn't do for her. Plus, you and April are happy; you have beautiful children and the perfect life, from what I can see.

First of all, don't believe everything you see. And yes, April is beautiful, intelligent and a great mother to our children. When I say it out loud, that should be enough for me to be the happiest man in the world. In reality, it isn't; I don't exactly know what it is, but it eats away at me daily, and I think April can feel it.

Man, that's that hoe in you; you just can't get enough pussy, and that's ironic since you're a Gynecologist. What kind of profession is that for a man anyway? It seems perverted for a man to have a profession in women's health. Isn't that what Bill Cosby did in the show? Now, look at his perverted ass.

Having to explain this to John for the millionth time, I begin my defense; Heathcliff Huxtable was a Gynecologist, Bill Cosby is a comedian and actor.

John rolls his eyes, same thing nigga, he wrote some of that shit in his shows, so some of the show's development came from his perverted mind.

Yeah, I get it. Trust me; sometimes it's weird as fuck. Having my hand in another man's wife's pussy while he's in the room looking over my shoulder; shit gets intense. On top of that, not all women have pretty pussies. Some women have odors, STDs and all types of shit. Just because it's pussy, doesn't mean it's all good.

Chris, be honest with me, I know we have our differences about marriage, and I've never asked you this mainly because it's not my business, but have you cheated on April?

After hesitating for a moment, I decided to open up a bit. You know what, I'll only entertain this question because you are my guy, and I want to give you a little insight into the decisions I've made. So, I will answer with an ambiguous maybe. But, I will tell you something most married men find true: having a side piece makes marriage more manageable. I know it sounds like some bullshit, but side chicks make life much easier for married men if the woman can accept being a side chick.

John hates hearing me say anything about being with another woman since he is so enamored with Apple. Chris, ain't nobody trying to listen to your hoe tactics. Side chicks are dangerous, they are distractions, and they destroy families.

Listen, after you get married, at least for me, things became too settled. We got stuck in everyday tasks, especially after having kids. Between taking out the trash, helping the kids with homework and making decisions on whether or not to get a new tile in the kitchen, everything other than fucking became more important topics. For me, having sex was like jumping double dutch; you have to time everything perfectly before jumping in. After a while, you might get head once in a blue moon for your birthday, and on top of that, your wife feels she's doing something special with that same old dry ass head she always gives. She doesn't even take the time to put on something sexy. Just a head wrap and slippers talking about, "are we gonna do this or not?" Now, side chicks my nigga, side chicks beg to suck your dick, her pussy is always wet, and they act like they are appreciative of having a nigga around. Side chicks give baths, roll blunts and make you feel like a king. They will rub your head, back and feet. They don't bog you down with petty things. Just give them some money for their hair and nails, pay a bill or two, and she'll be grateful. Every time you see them, you are the focus. For a man that's stressed with all the ills of the world, the mental peace they provide is priceless. So, when I go home to my wife, I'm able to endure the responsibilities of being a father and a husband and the sacrifice of myself for the betterment of the family. Because once you're married, the Bible is right, you become one person, and that one person is her. Everything has to be done her way, the way she likes it done, and if it's not done that way, hell is coming. Her wants become yours, her needs become your needs, and if you don't meet these requirements, you ain't shit, and you're not a good husband. So goes the creed of the simp beta male, happy wife, happy life. The truth is that most marriages fail because you never truly become one person. As an individual, you still have the hopes, goals and dreams you had when you were single; the difference is you'll have to sacrifice those things, at least some of them, to make your wife happy.

Chris, you bugging. If you wanna be a hoe, just be a hoe. Don't make excuses for your bullshit.

Shrugging and sipping champagne, maybe I am

tripping; I know society will tell me I am, but I know it's true, and it'll probably be the death of me.

Chris, always remember, if you don't heal from the trauma that causes this behavior, your past will always be your present. You must heal from the mental trauma you've endured that gives you that thought or you will never put your childish toys away for manhood. Maybe you should put that champagne down because you tripping, bruh.

Laughing, ain't nothing in my champagne but bubbles, my nigga. You asked me a question and I told you my answer. But, you're right, I am tripping because this is your wedding day, and I shouldn't be telling you all this bullshit. Apple has been a beautiful person ever since we've met, and I have nothing bad to say about her; she is a perfect choice for you.

Honestly Chris, I hear you, bruh. I'm sorry you're having problems within yourself, and now that I know, we will work through them. I've had problems dealing with a few issues and I know it's tough going through it alone. War takes a physical and mental toll on the soul of a man. Some of those tolls can never be mended, but Apple has always been there for me; she's loyal and deserves the best of me. I set aside my lusts and sexual desires a long time ago. I vow to let no harm come to her because she is my peace, and there is nothing I wouldn't do to protect her.

Damn, slow down killa. Save that shit for your vows because that was some touching shit, my dude. Shit, I want to marry you.

Whatever nigga, I mean that shit with everything inside me.

Okay, Derrick Jaxn, Tony Gaskins looking ass nigga, a woman is king and should be worshipped at all cost looking ass nigga. I got it, to each his own. I'm not here to judge you, and I hope you don't judge me either.

No doubt, you are my brother, and I love you Chris.

As we embrace with a handshake and a hug, there's a knock on the door. The wedding planner comes into the room. She informs us it's time to take pictures. She needs the groom and groomsmen in the main hallway.

Okay, we'll be right there. I turn and straighten John's tie and roll the lent brush over him. I love you too, you are my brother, and no matter what happens, I got your back.

Say less; real things don't need saying; they are felt, you

have always been real with me, and I'll always be there for you.

We continue the embrace for a moment and head out the door to meet up with the other groomsmen for pictures.

Hey John, go ahead and round up the other fellas; I need to stop by the bathroom first. Okay, hurry up. I'll meet you in the main hall.

Aight cool.

When I turn the corner, I see Apple walking down the hallway. She sees me, calls my name and gestures for me to come talk to her. My God, she looks amazing. She always looks amazing. Although April is the love of my life, Apple has definitely been the mistress of my mind. I know it's shitty of me because she's John's girl, but I can't count the number of times I've fucked the shit of Apple in my mind. Since grade school, John, Apple, April, and I have been close friends. We grew up in the same neighborhood, graduated from high school together. Apple and I have a friendship outside of John and April, so I didn't want to confuse her kindness with flirting, but I can't say she never felt a nigga.

Moreover, I didn't want to mess things up with April by

over playing my hand and making a play for Apple. I've dreamed, and I've wondered if things were different, if John wasn't my boy and April not my girl, if I could be the love of her life or is it just a lust thing. Although I have these thoughts, they are only thoughts, and things are not different, so I try to keep my distance, plus, John would kill me if he knew I had these thoughts.

Chris! Do you hear me talking to you?

After realizing I was starring, yeah, yeah, of course, Apple. What's up? You look amazing, by the way.

Thanks, Chris, you clean up well too. How's your boy holding up?

Ugh, actually, he ran out, and now I have to marry you according to the best man's code. Laughing, boy, you crazy, plus I don't think April would like that.

Nah, I'm bullshitting; he's great and excited about marrying you, of course.

Yeah, I'm excited too; I can't wait to marry John. He's amazing, and I'm lucky to be his bride.

We are both lucky to have John in our lives; you both are great people and great friends, and I couldn't be happier for both of you. But if you'd excuse me, I have to use the bathroom before we take these pictures.

Okay, handle your business, but I want to talk to you later. After John and I return from the honeymoon, I have something I want to talk to you about.

Okay, just let me know.

Now, I've heard the expression; she takes my breath away but seeing Apple in that dress gave me a clear vision of what the statement means. Standing in the stall pissing, I think to myself; I literally can't breathe when I look at her. Even when I look at my wife, I don't get the feeling I have when I look at Apple. I know I shouldn't feel this way. She's my best friend's soon-to-be wife, but damn, I can't help myself. I finish in the stall, wash my hands and hit the door.

When I get to the hall where the pictures are being taken, John shouts, where you been nigga? It doesn't take that long to piss.

When you are handling heavy artillery, it can take a while. I'm sure none of you niggas understands.

Unamused, John continues, bring yo goofy face ass on up here so we can finish with these pictures and get on with this wedding.

CHAPTER 2

The wedding went off without a hitch. The vows were given, the rice was thrown, and the doves released. After the wedding, the married couple was taken away to the reception in a white stretch Mercedes limo. April and I, along with the rest of the wedding party, followed in a sprinter van behind them. We sang the songs we loved during the reception, danced like we were kids again, and drank like we were in college. It was the best time I've had in a while. It felt good not to think about my issues with April, my career or my children. My only concern was to focus on making sure my guy didn't have to worry about anything. John was happy, Apple was beautiful, and the night couldn't have been better. As the night was ending, John pulled me to the side and reminded me he wanted to talk to me about something important.

Aye, Chris, I know we couldn't get into it tonight with the wedding going on, but we definitely need to talk.

Ok, cool, whenever you ready, hit me up. Whatever you need, just let me know.

Aight, I'm going to hit you up later this morning. Apple and I are leaving for our honeymoon, so we will take an Uber to the airport.

Uber? I'd never heard of it. Call me in the morning, and I'll take y'all to the airport. I have some things to do at the office, which will help me get my ass up.

Are you sure? I don't want to put you out, and we can't be late.

My guy, if you can't trust your boy, who can you trust? Don't worry about anything; I'm going to get y'all to the airport on time, no problem, so you and Apple can go, have fun, and hopefully make a baby. We can talk as soon as you get back, that's my word.

Okay, cool, 7:30 AM. Gripping my hand and looking straight into my eyes, I knew this nigga was serious. Be on time.

No doubt, I'll be here.

We dap, hug and part ways. I'd had too many drinks by this time, and April didn't feel comfortable driving; therefore, we left the car at the hotel and called for an Uber to take us home. We sat in the lobby for about 20 minutes before the Uber arrived at the hotel. I don't know what April had to drink or what was on her mind, but she was on one.

April started; what were you and John talking about outside the reception hall?

Nothing really; he was just saying he needed to talk. They are leaving for their honeymoon in the morning, so I told him we would talk when he got back.

We need to take a trip, sort of another honeymoon. Mom can keep the kids, and we can go somewhere and reconnect.

In my mind, I'm thinking, what in the hell is she talking about? We just talked about divorcing; now she is talking about vacations?

Side eyeing, I answer, yeah, babe, that sounds good.

I'm serious, Chris. It'll be fun; let me remind you why you once loved me. Once loved you? You are the mother of my children; I will always love you.

I know you love the mother of your children but do you love me? Before the money, the houses, cars, vacations and children, it was you and me, our dreams, our goals and a whole lot of sex. Remember that baby? Remember how you used to love this pussy, lust for this pussy, even married a nigga for this pussy? Laughing... amusing only herself.

Of course, I love pussy. I am a Gynecologist; it's my job to love it.

Don't play with me. You know what the fuck I mean. I'm talking about this pussy.

I open my eyes and look toward April; she opens her coat and lifts her dress. She has either removed her panties or didn't wear any, but she obviously wants my attention flashing her vagina at me.

What the hell are you doing? We are in the middle of a hotel lobby. Put that thang up.

I can tell she is getting heated at this point. I'm not sure if it's the alcohol or the opportunity, but she wants to express her feelings. She sits up and looks straight at me.

That's the problem; I see the way you look at other women. I see you lusting for those Instagram model women with the fake asses, fake tits and the fake desire to want your dumb ass, and I see the way you look at Apple.

Don't start that shit, April!

Don't start what shit, Chris? Don't start telling the truth? Ok then, tell me you don't want to fuck Apple. Tell me you don't lust for her. Tell me you don't want to be with her at all. Tell me you wouldn't risk everything to be with her.

Damn, she's right. I probably would risk everything for Apple. I know the way I feel is a violation of the two people I love the most in the world, but I can't help the way I feel about Apple. At this point, I'm definitely not being honest with April or myself. Fuck, where the hell is that Uber?

Come on, April, I think you've had too much to drink, and you're starting to say things that you may regret later.

I know what the fuck I'm saying. Don't make it seem as if I'm crazy. It's not the alcohol; I know you; I know you better than you know you. I knew you when you didn't know you. Tell me the truth, do you still love me? Not as the mother of your children but as your lover, partner and friend, do you love me as your wife?

Attempting to distract her from continuing this conversation, I lash out and grab her by the face. Keep your fucking voice down. This is not the place for this discussion. We can talk about it when we get home.

Snatching away from me, April continues, Nah, we ain't talking about shit when we get home. I already know the answers. It hurts knowing you're too much of a coward to tell me the truth.

A coward? How am I a coward?

Tears begin streaming down her face... You're a coward because you're selfish; you only care about yourself, your wants and your needs without considering other people you hurt like me, John and your kids.

If truth be told, she does deserve an explanation. But am I a coward for not expressing my feelings? In my mind, I'm protecting her by not telling her about the ill feelings I have about her, this marriage and Apple.

Although she deserves the truth, not even on my death bed will she ever hear it from me. Luckily, the phone rings, the Uber app alerts us the driver is outside. April turns away from me, walks out the lobby toward the parking lot and gets in the truck. I get in behind her, and we pull off from the hotel. During the ride home, April was quiet. I knew she was fuming from the heated conversation in the hotel lobby. I wanted to let her know I heard what she said, and I was open to talking about her feelings. I reached over to put my hand on her thigh. She doesn't push it away, so she seems open to conversation.

Yes, baby, I remember the days when the struggle was real. Your thighs helped a nigga through a lot of tough nights. I remember not having much and leaning on you for mental and physical support. All we had was each other. I knew you had my back, and I held you down. Trust me; I love you as my wife, partner, and friend. You have been the best wife a man could hope for, and I don't regret anything we've built together. Honestly, I wish I could tell you I'm the same person I was in those days, but I'm not. I don't know what happened to that person. I love the life we've built with our children, the family we've created, and I will always do everything I can to protect us. Although I miss the way we were, I don't know what happened to that person I was then, or maybe I've always been this person.

What person are you, Chris? Because I don't know this nigga. Whenever you find Chris with a family to take care of, let me know because that's the nigga I love. You know what, I'm going to take the kids to see my mom this weekend. That'll give you some time to think and figure out what you want from me and this marriage.

She adjusts her leg, pushing my hand away from her thigh. By this time, we are pulling up to the front of the house. We exit the truck, and April goes into the house. I tip the driver and give him five stars on the app. Instead of going straight into the house, I turn, look at the house and think to myself, I can't believe the life I live now. I mean, who would have guessed a boy from Meridian, Mississippi, would amass so much. I'm truly blessed and humbled by the thought. I go into the garage, roll and fire up a blunt. I look around the garage. We own a Tesla, Range Rover, motorcycles, and a boat I've never used. I can fit my entire childhood home inside here. Open land for as far as I can see, zero crime rate, an educational system where my children will have all the advantages to life and a wife that's fine as fuck, actually a woman that's out of my league. I am the American dream and my ancestors' dream that died in slavery, praying for a better future for their children. If I didn't have the potential to provide this way, there's no way April would've fucked me, I am so blessed, but with all these blessings, all I can think about is fucking Apple. What the fuck is wrong with me? I take a few more pulls from the blunt, put it out, let the garage down and walk in the house. I enter the den area; I can see the nanny on the couch asleep in the living room. I head up the stairs and peak in the kid's rooms. The kids were sleeping; I walked down the hallway to the bedroom. April had just gotten out of the shower because the room was steamy, and her clothes were on the floor. As I began taking off my clothes, I heard the bathroom door open. April came out wrapped in a towel and her hair tied back. It could've been the weed, but she seemed to be walking in slow motion like in a music video. As this moment continued in slow motion, I said to myself, damn, my wife is fine as fuck. Her legs are long like a runway model with nice strong calves and pretty toes. She turns, enters her shoe room and drops her towel. Her body is still in great shape; after two kids, her stomach is flat with a faint six pack emerging, defined arms and shoulders with those titties looking succulent. For a 24-year-old woman, she is amazing, but at age 40, with two kids, her body is spectacular. Now, for my favorite part of the show, that ass. Standing there, I watched the bounce of her ass, the curve of her hips, the thickness of her thighs and the arch in her back as the towel fell to the ground. As she finishes oiling her body, I walk up behind her and begin kissing her neck while gripping her breast. She turns towards me, confused, hurt and with pain in her eyes. I hate seeing her this way, especially knowing I was the cause. Again, I kissed her lips. She was cold and unresponsive. I pulled her closer, looked deeper into her eyes and continued kissing her lips. She closes her eyes, raises her arms to wrap them around my neck. It felt like an eternity since we've been in this space. I continued kissing her lips and squeezing her ass. We continued kissing from the shoe room back into the bedroom area; I walked her over to the bed and laid her down on her back. I left no spot untouched from her lips to her neck around her nipples down to her naval. I continued kissing past her waist into her glory. She grabs the back of my head and wraps her thighs over my shoulders, pulling me closer, inviting me inside her comfort. As I continue kissing her inner thigh, she lets out short, inhaled breathes, anticipating the arrival of pleasure. My tongue circles around her vulva as I kiss her labia. Her breath became deeper, her moans more intense as I sucked the clitoris and licked inside her walls. She begins to scream out, gripping my head tighter and holding me in the place she loves until she climaxes over and over again. I turn her over onto her stomach, spread her ass cheeks and handle business with the groceries. You feel me, right? I make my way back to her spine, kissing her waist, the small of her back, sucking on her sides, massaging her shoulders and caressing her neck. I roll her onto her back, lift her thighs back onto my shoulders and penetrate her slowly, gently and lovingly. As I enter her body, her body tenses then relaxes to allow me fully inside her. My long, thick, engorged penis continues to penetrate her body as I lay flat on top of her; I listen to her breathe deeper, gasping and moaning as I keep thrusting deeper inside her soul. Every stroke inside her goes harder and deeper; sweat trickles down her face, her moans become screams, we both climax as I release inside her womb.

Looking at me confused and satisfied, April says, "Damn, where did that come from?" Laughing, you know I'm good for at least one dick down a year.

Nah, I forgot; it's been so long, but damn I needed it.

The sex was amazing, and if only for one night, I remembered, April is my wife, and she is the woman I'm committed to love. For the first time in a long time, we laughed, talked to each other, not at each other and enjoyed this moment together. After laying and talking with April, my phone vibrates on the desk. I walk over the phone, look at the number...oh shit, it's Apple. "We need to talk."

CHAPTER 3

A s I lay in bed after having the best night in a long time with my wife, April, I began to reflect on the beginning of our relationship. In the beginning, there was nothing I wouldn't do to get her attention. I would call her 4-3 times a day. We would talk for hours about nothing until the early morning, knowing I had class or work the next morning. I couldn't imagine a day without her being a part of it back then. Now, when I see her number on my phone, I cringe to answer, knowing it's either something wrong or some other bullshit I need to do or didn't do or not doing enough to satisfy her needs. The 4-3 daily phone calls were reduced to 2-1 text messages a week. And, it's never about good shit like come home and fuck the shit out of me. It's usually, why the fuck did you do this or why the fuck didn't you do that. But tonight was good; I remember this woman, I remember who I am, and I remember my purpose for her and this family.

Suddenly, I hear my phone buzzing. I pull my arm from under April, turn over and reach for my phone on the nightstand. Wiping my eyes to clear my vision, I read the text; it's from Apple. The message read, "Can we talk?" My thoughts begin to race a bit because, for one, it's her wedding night, and for two, what the hell could she want to talk about. I look back at April to see if she's still asleep. The phone didn't wake her, so she's still asleep with her back turned to me in a spooning position. I sit up in the bed, pull the covers back, grab my phoned and walk down the stairs into the bathroom in the guest room. I close the door to text Apple back. "Yeah, hmu." Almost immediately, the phone vibrates, I answer...

Hey, what's up? Everything ok?

Yeah, everything is good. I know you were supposed to take us to the airport this morning, but there's been a change of plans.

Can you come over so we can talk? Talk to who?

Chris, who the fuck you think? Us nigga. You, John and I. Something has come up, and we need to talk to you. Just come over to the house. We can sit down and talk through some things.

Apple and I are cool, but this doesn't sound right. John would never allow Apple to call me to talk about something. Not that he's jealous-hearted, he's a private man and would never put Apple at the forefront of him calling me for anything. Suspectantly, I reply, Put John on the phone.

John gets on the phone. Surprisingly, his voice is cracking like he's been crying. Hey, Chris, we are postponing the honeymoon. I know this sounds funny, and I promise I wouldn't call you on some bullshit this early in the morning, but we have to have this conversation today as soon as possible. I need your help.

Say no more; I'll be there in about an hour. I hang up the phone, and my mind begins to turn. After hearing the tone of their voices, I'm beginning to have a bad feeling about this urgent conversation that needs to be had with me immediately. What's so important for them to postpone their honeymoon trip? What in the hell is deep enough for John to be crying? I've never heard nor seen John cry about anything.

After going through several scenarios in my head, nothing made sense. I walk back up the stairs to the master bedroom, open the door, and April is sitting up in the bed, looking at her phone. She looks up at me and says, why is Apple texting me looking for you?

I'm not sure yet; I just got off the phone with Apple and John. John said he needed my help with something, but he didn't want to discuss it over the phone. I was supposed to take them to the airport this morning. Apparently, they've had a change of plans, so I told him I would come over to their house and talk about it.

Are they not going on their honeymoon?

Nah, I guess not. John sounded different on the phone. I've never heard him like this before. Sounds like they need money again. I know that's your boy, but when's enough enough?

Don't do that, April. John is my friend, my brother, please don't start that again.

Chris, you know I'm right. You've paid for the man's wedding and honeymoon. A honeymoon that they aren't going on. You can't be this blind. All I'm saying is don't let him continue to use you.

CHRISTOPHER PEOPLES | 29

Alright April, maybe you're right, but what am I supposed to do if John needs help. You know how we grew up. We grew up with nothing. I prayed and worked my ass off to be able to provide for everyone I love.

I understand the survivor's guilt is real, and just because you can provide for everyone doesn't mean you should be used. Listen, you are a good and just man. It's a burden that will always weigh heavy on your head, but it's not on you to save everyone.

I understand your concern, and anything I provide John will never deprive you or the kids of anything. I'm trying to make sure everyone is good. If money is the one thing keeping them from happiness, then I don't want to keep them from it because God knows we all could use some happiness.

Disappointed with me, April says, okay, whatever, Chris. I'll text Apple and let her know.

After showering and getting dressed, I walk over to the bed. April has gone back to sleep. I kiss her on the cheek and let her know I'm leaving the house and will be back after I leave the office. Before I leave, I look in on the kids, grab a piece of fruit and reset the alarm on the way out. While waiting for the car to warm a bit, I fired up a blunt to relieve some of the anxiety I was experiencing about this conversation. Without any clue about the subject of this conversation, my nerves are on edge. After about 10 minutes, I back out the driveway and head towards John's crib.

When I pull up to John's house, I sit in the driveway for a moment. Replaying what April said in my head, I am determined not to come off any money during this conversation. With my mindset and a game plan in place, I get out of the car and walk up to the door. Before I could knock, Apple opened the door.

Come in, Chris; I'm glad you were able to make it.

I was captivated by what she was wearing when she arrived at the door. She's wearing a crop top with her midriff exposed and boy shorts with half her ass revealed. She reaches out and hugs me around the neck tightly. This is unusual because she normally offers me a side hug or gives me the church hug with her ass poked out. You know the hug with a distance between our bodies, so there are no misunderstandings. This time, her titties were pressed against my chest, forcing my hands down around the small of her back because of our height difference, joining right above her ass crack.

Looking over her shoulder, I notice her ass cheeks bouncing as she stands on her toes to reach my neck. After a longer than normal damn near erotic hug, my dick starts to stiffen. She pulled away from me quickly after noticing my dick was poking her in the stomach.

Smiling, Apple continues, John is in the back; he'll be out in a minute. Do you want anything? Juice, soda or water? I can make you breakfast if you want.

Make breakfast? I didn't know you could cook. There's a lot you don't know about me.

Is that right? Who taught you how to cook?

Well, if you must know. My mom taught me to cook. She's a great cook, a world-renowned cook. World-renowned huh?

Yeah, before I moved to Meridian, we lived in Chicago. I lived there until I was almost 12 years old. As you know, my mom is originally from Meridian, but when she moved to Chicago, she took over a restaurant that has been in our family for generations.

What did the restaurant serve?

We served what northerners would call southern comfort food like oxtails, collard greens and cornbread.

We also had the best pies.

Mouth watering, I say, Wow, I would love some good pot roast, mashed potatoes and sweet potato pie.

Apple continues, My mom loved desserts; obviously, a love she passed on to me evidenced by this big ole ass I carry around with me.

Nah, I haven't noticed you carrying ass around.

Whatever nigga, laughing, she continues. My grandmother told me my mom would eat apple pie every night while pregnant with me. Therefore, my grandmother named me Apple from my mom's love for the dessert pie.

Okay, I didn't know that about you. I guess you learn something new every day. As I said, Chris, there's a lot you don't know about me. So, how about breakfast? Although I am intrigued, I'll have to take a rain check.

Aight, maybe I will cook for you one day soon.

Sounds good; I'm looking forward to it. Anyways, where's John? Tell him to bring his ass out here.

Okay, but before I tell him you're here, I want to tell you, this is hard for him. It's hard for us to ask this of you. Whatever we discuss here must stay between us; when I say us, I mean me, you and John, not April. And some parts of this, just me and you.

I sit there as I hear the words coming out her mouth; it's hard for me to comprehend the meaning of this warning. Listen, Apple, respectfully, unless we are talking about fucking, there's nothing I don't tell April and John. So, unless we are talking about fucking, what the fuck are we talking about?

She smiles again, turns and starts walking away, stops, looks back and says, "we talking about fucking."

Before I could pick my jaw up off the floor, she turned back around and walked towards the back room. As she walks away, her ass sways, dances and claps as her thighs move each cheek up and down with every step. Every time I see Apple, it's like she is moving in slow motion, the background fades, and Juvenile's "Slow Motion" plays in my head. Finally, she disappears into the room of darkness while I sit there with only my thoughts. What the fuck are these people up to today? At this point, I'm creeped out and damn near uncomfortable but extremely curious. Apple has never played with me through high school and college about us getting together. Even when John was overseas doing tours with the military, she never wavered, at least not to my knowledge. After sitting there for about 10 minutes, John comes from the back room and sits at the table with me. John looks like he sounded on the phone, vulnerable, desperate and afraid. He obviously hasn't slept, and he's been drinking as he reeked of whiskey.

What's up, Chris? I'm glad you were able to make it this morning. How's April and the kids?

Nigga, you act like I didn't just see you yesterday, at your wedding, which we just left about 5 hours ago. I'm tired; I had a good night, but I got some shit to do at the office, and I'm ready to go back to my bed, so if you would please tell me what's going on here.

Aight, straight to business then. To explain what's going on, I have to tell you something I've never shared with you. During my second tour of duty, I was working on a mission to move some inventory from the base to a training site. We encountered an ambush of sorts during the transition and were forced to trade fire to protect the inventory and our lives. Amid this battle, I took two bullets to my pelvic area. The bleeding was uncontrollable; I lost a lot of blood and nearly my life. Since that time, I've had several surgeries. Unfortunately, I could never recover what I've lost. The thing I've lost is the ability to provide the one thing my now wife wants the most. Due to my injuries, I can't get an erection; therefore, I cannot impregnate my wife. Over the years, I've had 10 surgeries, the surgeries were expensive, I was dropped from my insurance coverage, and consequently, I've depleted our savings. Basically, we have nothing left. If you hadn't paid for the wedding, I don't know if we would've had a wedding. The truth is, I'm exhausted.

After a short pause John continues, I'm exhausted with having surgeries, I'm tired of Apple pressuring me to have children, and I'm exhausted with feeling less than a man due to this issue. After hours of discussion and prayer, I've agreed to have one more surgery. Apple found this doctor in Nashville specializing in regenerative tissue. The procedure has reversed the condition I'm experiencing. Once again, the procedure is expensive, it's not 100% it'll work, but I'm willing to put myself through this one more time for Apple. There it is; this is why we've asked you to come over for this conversation. As I've said, the procedure is expensive, and we need to ask you to finance this surgery. I've taken several loans, and we can barely make the monthly payments. Like I said on the phone, I need your help.

By the time John finished the story, Apple had returned to the table and sat next to John. I sat there stunned for a moment. With my head buried in my hands, contemplating and digesting everything I was just told, I couldn't believe it. I couldn't believe what John had gone through over the years, and I had absolutely no idea.

John reaches over and places his hands on my shoulder; bruh, so what are you thinking?

As I lift my head from my hands, I begin to cry. I feel sorry hearing my brother has been in so much pain. I can't believe you've kept this from me for all this time. How could you go through something like that without telling me?

At the time, you were in school and starting your family. I didn't want to burden you with my problems.

You could've come to me; nothing comes before family.

I'm sorry for not telling you earlier; honestly, I'm embarrassed. It's not easy telling anyone your dick doesn't work. You know what I'm saying?

Yeah, I know what you're saying; I guess it is tough to admit that shit, but you still could've told me. I look over at Apple; tell me more about this doctor in Nashville. What's the procedure she'll provide for John?

Apple gets up from the table, walks over to the desk and pulls out a procedure brochure. Apple, what do you think about all this?

Apple looks over at John, hesitated a moment before answering the question. The truth is, Chris, I'm tired of seeing him go through these surgeries, but it's important to me to have children. Apple reaches over and squeezes John's hand; it's important to me to have children. You and April have a beautiful family, and I want the same for us. But, as John said, the surgery is expensive, and it's not guaranteed to work. I figure the best way to save the expense of the surgeries, physically, mentally and financially, is to do it the old-fashioned way. Chris, I want you to impregnate me.

Immediately, John became irate and jumped up from the table. What? Hell no, hell fucking no, Apple! I told you don't bring that shit up. What the fuck are you talking about? Chris, if you even think about fucking Apple, I'll murder you where you stand. Apple, get the fuck out of here with that shit. No fucking way!

Calm down, brother; we are just talking through our

options. She was only giving her opinion. Sit back down, and let's continue discussing this.

John continues pacing around the room like a lion stalking his next meal. Ain't shit else to talk about. Seems all at once John's demeanor changes; I know you love this shit, Chris. You've wanted to fuck Apple ever since we were in high school. You think I didn't fucking know?

Know what? I've never made a play for Apple. Bruh, you tripping. You asked me over here to talk about this; I had no idea she would suggest that. Hell, I didn't know anything about any of this shit until right now.

It doesn't matter, Chris. She knows, and you know how I feel about that shit. I asked you here to explain my situation and ask you to help me pay for this surgery; that's it.

Okay, John, calm down. Listen, you're right. How much do you need to have the surgery? Disgusted, John leaves the room with tears streaming down his face.

Apple leaves the room behind.

As I sit in the room alone, again, I can't believe the shit I just heard from John. He's always been overbearing of

Apple, and he never liked us talking or being around each other. It all makes sense now. Apple wants me to impregnate her? All this time, John was scared I would fuck Apple because of his insecurities about his physical situation. My mind is blown.

After putting together some pieces of this puzzle, I grab my jacket and head out the door. I'm fuming by the time I get to my car. I can't believe what was just said. How did we start talking about fucking and end with me plotting for his wife? I get in the car, slam the door and push start the car. I reach in the ashtray and fire up the remainder of the blunt I rolled on the way over. By this time, Apple comes jogging towards the car; she looks in the window, walks around the car and opens the passenger door. She closes the door and reaches for me to pass her the blunt. She hits it a couple of times and hands it back.

Listen, Chris, I know John is having difficulty hearing this, but he'll come around. I am going to keep talking to him about this, but I wanted to know how you are feeling about it.

Which part are you asking about? Us fucking or paying for the surgery? Well, I was talking about you impregnating me.

I'm not sure. I couldn't have a child and not be a father, plus John would be crushed by knowing I'm the father of his child. His pride seems beaten down enough.

So, you rather pay for the surgery than fuck me?

It's not that; I'd love to fuck you but not like this. Text me later with the amount of the procedure, and I'll have my accountant wire the money to his account in the morning.

Thank you, but that's not all I'm talking about. Even if the surgery works, it's less than a 2% chance his sperm will produce a child; with all the damage caused in his accident, he'll be extremely lucky to get an erection. I set up the consultation for this weekend. That'll give us a chance to get, let's say, acquainted. John's right, I know you've wanted this pussy for a while; here's your chance, don't miss it.

Apple, listen to what are you asking me to do? John is my brother; he's lost enough; his pride is all he has left. I don't want to see him hurting. Even if you talk him into this, think about what he's giving up for your happiness.

I don't want to hurt John either; I love John, he's everything I've ever wanted, but he promised me everything. If you do this, it will complete our family. She leans over the seat, kisses me on the ear and whispers, it's only one night, one time, and we never have to speak of this again. I'll call you when everything is in place. She backs away and gets out of the car.

FUCK!

CHAPTER 4

I hadn't heard from John or Apple in a few days when I received a text from Apple as I was getting ready for work.

Is everything good? What are your plans for the evening?

I text back; I'm not sure yet. April and the kids are going out of town, but I don't know when they're leaving out.

John just left for Nashville for the consultation. He won't be back until Monday morning, so I'm going to cook, have some wine and chill. Can you keep me company?

I replied, Apple, I'm not sure I'm 100% comfortable

doing this. I'll let you know later if I'm available.

April and the kids are going away to her mother's house for the weekend, and with John being away in Nashville, this seems to be a perfect time. The nanny is off because the kids will be gone, so I'll be home alone this weekend as well.

Before leaving for work, I spoke with April about her plans to leave her mom's house. What time are you leaving for your mom's crib?

The kids have a half-day at school. I think we will leave around 3 pm. I want to make it to Meridian before it gets dark.

That's a good idea, I'm going to close the office early, and I'll be home to see you guys off.

Really? That'll be great. Another thing, since you're being so nice, do you mind picking up the kids on your way home?

No problem, I'd love to pick them up.

Don't take them to McDonald's; I'm going to make lunch, and we are going to take mom out to dinner tonight, so don't spoil their appetites.

Cool, I'll try; you know I can't deny my babies.

We laugh about it, and I'm out the door. On this particular day, the sun was shining, no clouds in the sky, a light breeze was coming in from the west, and it was a brisk 65 degrees, no barking from the dog, no smog, for the Ice Cube fans. What I mean is today was, in my opinion, perfect. On my way to work, John calls.

I answer the phone; what's good, my brother?

What's up, bruh? Just letting you know I've made it to Nashville, and I'm scheduled to have the surgery in the morning.

No doubt, I'm praying for you and don't worry about anything; the money is in your account, so you're covered.

Thanks, man. Hey, listen, Apple is home alone this weekend. Go over and check on her for me. Whatever happens, no regrets, and don't think about me at all. She wants this, and I need you to do this for me, to keep my marriage together.

I mumble in a low, wimping tone, hey man, we don't...

Listen to me, Chris, you are a good dude, a good husband, a good father and doing this for me proves you're a good friend, my brother. But let's not play games, I see the way you look at Apple, and I can only imagine the thoughts you've had about her, don't front. And it's okay, she's an incredible woman, and she deserves her desires to be fulfilled. If not you, then it'll probably be some dude I don't know. If it has to happen, I want it to be you.

Okay, I understand, don't worry about that and focus on getting through this procedure. I'm going to check on Apple. Just make sure you take care of yourself, and I'll see you when you get home. I love you, brother.

Love you too, brother, see you soon.

Still driving to work and in deep thought about the conservation with John, my phone vibrates, scaring the shit out of me. It's Apple.

Hey you, did you forget about me?

Nah, I didn't forget about you. What did you say you were cooking?

We continue to text back and forth for several minutes throughout the morning. We finished with me saying everything was good and the plan for tonight would work for me. She responded how she was looking forward to the evening and for me to come over around 9 pm. I let her know that sounded good, and I'll see her later tonight. Usually, I'm a cool individual; this situation has me shaken. I ain't never scared, but some situations make me nervous, this is one of those situations.

Throughout the morning, I continued to struggle with this decision, am I really going to fuck my best friend's wife? I could just give John the money and hope the surgery works. On the other hand, he asked me for this favor, and honestly, I damn sure want to do it. But am I doing this for them or me? I usually turn to John when I have major decisions, but I already know his answer. Either way, I'm doing what's right, right?

When I got to the office, my schedule was jammed. I barely had time to breathe. After the morning portion of clients, I was winding down because I was leaving early to pick up my children from school. I closed the door to my office, leaned back in the chair and attempted to close my eyes for a moment to meditate on the rest of my evening. The conversation with John and Apple continues to have my head swimming. Although I told Apple I'd be over later, I wasn't completely sure if I would go through with it. Just as I drift away for a nap, my secretary buzzes me to tell me there was a young lady in the lobby to see me. She's saying she knows me, doesn't have an appointment but wants to see me. After a small hesitation a quick peek at the office cameras, I came out of the office and looked around the room. I didn't see anyone. I turned back into my office when I saw Apple coming from around the corner. Damn, Apple is such a breath of fresh air. Every time I see her, she takes my breath away, and today, she is stunning as usual. She was dressed in one of those little, free-flowing, short sundresses I love seeing women wear, and a pair of heels that makes her ass shake like a crackhead in rehab. After shaking off the weird stare from my secretary, an awkward look of surprise and delight overcame my face.

Hey, Apple, what's up? What are you doing here?

Hey Chris, she reaches out and hugs me. What's wrong, you not happy to see me?

My bad, you just caught me off guard. What can I do for you? I was in the area, and I wanted to talk to you.

Yeah, of course, come into my office.

Speaking to my secretary, have the Nurse Practitioner see the next client and let me know when Mrs. Edwards

CHRISTOPHER PEOPLES | 49

is here. Thanks.

Closing the door to my office, I turn to Apple and invite her to take a seat. She takes a seat on the couch and crosses her legs. My head starts to race a bit. What the fuck is she doing here? There's little chance she is just in the area because my office is far from where she lives with John.

So, Apple, what can I do for you?

She starts with; I'm here for an examination. An examination?

Well yeah, since we are about to have a baby, I figured it's best if I'm seen by the best OBGYN in the state, right?

Wait, what are you talking about? I haven't agreed to anything yet.

I knew you were full of shit. Maybe you need some inspiration. You said you'd do anything for John, anything for family, right?

Feeling a bit disgusted and excited, I pause before continuing. Lord knows I want to fuck the core out of Apple but not like this. "Of course, I'll do anything for John. This doesn't feel right. Besides, don't you already have an OBGYN? It's true, I am the best, but your doctor can examine you and send me the notes if you want me to review them."

Yes, I do. She's out of town, and we don't have time to wait for her to return.

Looking down and away from me, I know she's running game, but I'm willing to see how far she takes it. She continues, she postponed my last appointment, and I'm due for my annual checkup. Can you check me out?

Does John know you are here? Because you know he'll kill us both, right? Yes, he does know I'm here. What? Does he make you nervous?

A little...

Do you ask the other ladies here if their husbands know where they are?

No, I know your husband, and that mutherfucka is crazy. He said he would kill me for touching you.

Standing up from the couch, Apple replies, I think we both know, that's not gonna happen. I know you spoke to John today, and he told me you were on board with this.

The picture is becoming a bit clearer about this visit from Apple. After a slight agreement about John knowing where she is, she walks towards the examination table, climbs on it and puts her legs in the stirrups. Her dress raises to her waist, exposing she didn't wear any panties. She begins rubbing the inside of her thighs and her vagina. Her pussy is pretty, shaped like a pear, her ass is shaped so perfectly, it'll make a queer nigga stop, look and stare. She looks at me and says, so can I get that examination?

Shaking with excitement, I quickly bitched out and attempted to extinguish the moment. Apple, listen, I'd love to continue this visit, but unless you can tell me what's going on, I'm going to have to ask you to leave; as you can see, I'm a little busy.

Okay, enough with the subliminal, I came here to fuck, let's call it a little pregame warm-up, if you will. You sounded a little shaky over the phone. I wanted you to see what it is and confirm your desires.

Confirm my desires?

Please nigga, you have to be the only one that doesn't know. Everyone knows you've always wanted to fuck me. I knew, John knows, shit, April knows. Why do you think I'm never invited to your house? I'm not invited often because you can't keep your tongue in your fucking mouth when I'm around.

Whatever. I'm not that bad, am I? Anyway, how did you get John to change his mind?

We talked and like I said, he wants me happy; this will make me happy. Therefore, I'm here to let you know if you're willing, I'm willing. If you're not, I hope April doesn't find out about this.

Clearing my throat and stuttering, what about April?

If I had an honest bone in my body, I would admit that I didn't give a damn how April felt about it. But I wanted Apple to make things okay because I didn't want the guilt. I didn't want to think about the hurt I'd bring to April nor her disappointment, knowing I failed her and our children. I was weak and needed an excuse to do something I may regret.

Apple continues, I can't speak for April; I'm sure she would be devastated if she found out, but, in this situation, I'm being selfish. I thought about asking her. But asking her if I could fuck her husband and have a child, out loud, shit sounds crazy as hell, she'd probably kick my ass. At this moment, all I can think about is having a piece of what she has, and I want a family.

She walks over to me, grabs the back of my neck, looks into my eyes with tears of pain and kisses me softly. She takes my hands and places them around her back onto her ass cheeks. Just as I imagined, her ass felt as soft as her lips. As the moment becomes more intense, she moves my hand around from her ass to her thighs onto her fat, warm, wet pussy. She takes my fingers out, places them in her mouth and sucks the tips. Do you wanna taste? She rubs her fingers against her pussy, I hear the suction from the wetness, and she places her fingers into my mouth; she asks, how does it taste?

Before I could answer, my phone buzzed, it was my secretary, breaking the tension building in the room. Dr. Simpson, Mrs. Edwards is here.

Thank you, let her know I'll be with her shortly. Turning my attention back to Apple, I want this to happen, but I never imagined I'd have an opportunity in a million years, nor did I think it would happen like this.

Apple, this shit is crazy.

Chris, I'm okay with this happening, and I want this to happen. Like I've said before, I love John, and there's nothing I wouldn't do for him, but I don't want to deceive you. John is hurting about this, and it tears him apart that he can't please me sexually. Shit, it tears me apart that he's unable to enjoy a sexual experience with me. But what am I to do? It's not about the money for me. I want this experience with you. I see how you look at me; I noticed the awkward tension between us. I can feel your attraction to me. Do you deny your attraction to me? Do you deny anything I've said so far? I guess what I need to know is, do you want this to happen?

More than anything, but I haven't quite decided yet, if I'm being honest. I am married to April, your friend, remember? Are you okay with that? Or I could just give John the money and hope the surgery can bring him back to normal.

In a bit of a rage, Apple raised up and stepped off the table, don't give me that I'm married shit. Yes, April is my friend, so you know I know y'all are having problems too, real marital problems, and I know y'all not fucking either, and your dick works, so, what'll it be, Chris? You could just give him the money, or you can give him the money and satisfy what we've both been looking to do.

Grabbing her stuff and walking toward the door, she turns and replies, the choice is yours, the ball is in your court or whatever cliché you want to quote. Apple's tone changes from seductive to focused as she walks towards me. You know my number. Let me know something soon. Talk to you later, Chris. Calmly, she kisses me on the lips and leaves my office.

CHAPTER 5

After seeing a few more clients, I tell my secretary I'm leaving for the day. I ask her to lock up after she leaves for the weekend. I get in my car and head to pick up my children from school. I saw my children walking toward the car as I approached the school. First thing out they mouth, yep, you guessed it.

Dad, can we stop by McDonald's?

No doubt, baby girl, anything you want. I turned and looked at my son, who seemed deep in thought and asked, little man, how was your day at school?

It was good.

You seem like something is on your mind; what's going on?

Nothing. It's just that all my friends were talking about this Kaepernick situation.

My son Chris Il or Jay is a 12-year-old future activist in the making. This kid has the most compelling insight on world topics I've ever heard from a child or an adult, for that matter. He's brilliant, a trait he definitely gets from me, of course.

What's the Kaepernick situation, son?

I hear people on TV argue the point of Kaepernick sitting for the National Anthem is disrespectful to the American flag. Then, they argued kneeling for the National Anthem is disrespectful, right?

That's right.

Kaepernick said he sat and kneeled to bring awareness to police brutality and unfair treatment by the police in urban neighborhoods, right?

Nodding in agreement, I respond, Black Americans have been treated poorly in this country for several hundreds of years; athletes like Muhammad Ali, Jim Brown, and LeBron James, amongst others, have done a lot to bring awareness to this truth. Kaepernick is carrying on the fight to bring the issue to light and using his NFL celebrity to enhance this message.

Yeah, but he's already a celebrity. When you say his name, you already think of NFL quarterback. Why mess with the NFL's money when they had nothing to do with police brutality? Now they look bad for something they actually support. The NFL sponsors programs in the Black community, which many minorities benefit from. They don't want to see Black people brutalized either, but they are making money in the entertainment business. He doesn't need the NFL to back him up. Why risk losing millions of dollars and your career for a cause that can be addressed on another platform. In my opinion, he played this wrong. The problem is he used the NFL's platform to broadcast his message and not his own.

How so, son?

It's like being invited into someone's home and yelling at their kids to clean their rooms and wash the dishes. Those things may need to be done, but who are you to go into someone else's home and tell them what to do with their kids? I think it's a distraction from the bigger issue.

Somewhat confused about where he was going with this, I ask, a distraction from what, son?

Police brutality is a major issue and needs to be addressed but the bigger issue is that the NFL is not his platform. Imagine if you owned a business that produces 8.1 billion dollars in annual revenue, and you have an employee causing a potential problem that has nothing to do with the business itself. Even though about 70% of NFL players are Black, most of the ad revenue, ticket sales, TV network deals are worked out between over 90% of White males. The NFL is not beating and killing Black Americans; matter of fact, the NFL has created the largest population of young Black millionaires, more than any other business, including Hollywood or the stock market.

Ok, that's great information, so what's the solution?

It's deeper than a solution, dad. There needs to be a plan and a process for individuals on the same page, pulling in the same direction. Kaepernick has millions of followers on Instagram, Facebook and other social media platforms and a community of popular individuals with the same number of followers or more. The solution is to build your platform and shout from it.

Wow, that's a sound argument, and I agree with your points. The thing you must understand son is that you are a Black male in America, and that alone makes you a target to be harassed, harmed or murdered by race soldiers, policemen or individuals who feel they are superior to you and judge you by only your skin color. At any time, for no reason or for reasons your white counterparts would get a slap on the wrist, you will not be given the same opportunity, and you will be punished to the fullest degree. Although we live in an affluent neighborhood and you will be afforded opportunities even most white kids will never see, you will still be seen as lesser, and you will have to work harder than your white friends, and sadly, in some people's minds, you will still be just a nigga. So, don't judge how Kaepernick protested or where he protested; focus on why he protested. It was so you; my beautiful Black son can shine as bright as you can, be judged on your works and how you treat others and not by your skin color alone. Maybe it's time to start working on your platform with a YouTube channel or blog. Your Uncle John is great at media relations; I'm sure he would love to work with you on that project.

Out of nowhere, my daughter screams from the backseat; that sounds great, but what's up with the

McDonald's stop? We've passed like three of them already!

Aw shit, my bad, baby, I'm stopping at the next one coming up.

We pull into the next McDonald's and order three Oreo McFlurry's. We sat and ate them. And sure enough, right on cue, Avery spills half the damn McFlurry on the seat of my brand-new Tesla. After wiping her down and attempting to get the ice cream off the seats, we headed toward the house. Screaming and cursing in my head and under my breath, we pull up to the house. I can see April standing in the driveway with her arms folded and a scowl on her face. The obvious "I'm mad" pose.

When I park the car, April opens the door for my daughter to get out of the car, and you know Avery outed me as soon as she got out of the car.

We went to McDonald's, mommy. I had ice cream.

Is that right? Daddy took you to McDonald's? Yes, daughter nods. That's great, go in the house and wash your face. I'll be upstairs in a moment to help you finish getting your things ready to go to Me'mo house.

As soon as the kids close the door to the house, April turns to me. I told you not to take the kids to McDonald's because I made lunch for them. I swear you do some dumb ass shit, Chris. You couldn't handle a simple request. What the fuck were you thinking? I hope whatever is going on with you gets cleared up soon. Why don't you take this weekend and think about what you really want from this marriage and this family? I scheduled an appointment to see the therapist next week. I've been going, and she wants you to join the next session. Can you at least do that for me? For us?

I wanted to say fuck no. The look in her eyes of pain and disappointment overcame my need to be confrontational at this time. I agreed, yeah, babe, I can do that; I'll join you in a session if it means something to you.

In April's mind, I'm sure she feels she's doing the right thing by trying to save our marriage through counseling sessions. Obliviously, she's hurting or missing something either I'm incapable of providing or don't want to provide. Unfortunately, neither one of us can communicate what we want from each other at this time. Sometimes it's helpful to say you're unhappy and start from there. Talk things out and try to find a way through the pain. To me, April is ungrateful for the life I've provided for her. She doesn't have to work, and she doesn't have to worry about money ever again. We have a beautiful home, beautiful kids, amazing friends and opportunities most White people would be jealous of. She talks down to me like I'm a child and incapable of handling my business or guiding this family.

On top of that, she continues to throw her bitch ass father in my face, who never achieved the professional or financial level I've achieved, but because he's a busted-ass pastor with an outdated perspective on human behavior, his opinion is more valid than mine? No fucking way. One thing is for sure; I want my respect.

After gathering myself with a freshly rolled blunt, I walk into the house. I see my kids scurrying through the house, gathering their last-minute toys to take to their grandmother's house. April is in the kitchen, gathering snacks and juice boxes for the trip. I ask if there is anything she needs me to do. She asks me to finish loading the truck and make sure Avery is buckled up. I respond, no problem and begin to hunt for my daughter. Finally, I coral her and the toys she wants to take on the trip. I begin moving toward the door and taking the items outside. I get the items in the truck along with Avery and Jay. I kiss them both and tell them I love them, and I'll see them when they get back. Avery asks, Dad, why are you not coming with us? April comes from around the house just in time to hear the question. April responds because he has things to do this weekend at home. Looking at me judgmentally, she gets in the truck and starts the engine. She rolls the window down and puckers like she wants a kiss; it feels more like a show for the kids. She kisses me and says she loves me, and off they go.

By this time, it's about 3 pm. I look at my phone; I have several text messages and emails but none from Apple. I take off my shoes and tie, get comfortable, pour a glass of Dusse and stretch out on the couch in my den. I fire up the blunt and take several pulls until my eyes get tight. I finish off the glass of Dusse and fall asleep. After a couple of hours passed, I woke up to the buzz of my phone. It's April telling me they've made it to Meridian safely, and she'll call me tomorrow. I respond, Okay. I check the time on my phone, it's a little past 7 pm, and I've received a couple of texts from Apple.

4:31 pm... Hey, you. Everything still good? 4:52 pm...

Still no word from you.

5:23 pm... Are you ok?

6:01 pm... Chris, are you flaking on me?

Finally, I text back...Hey Apple, sorry I was asleep, what you doing?

Apple responded in seconds. Waiting on you, baby, are you still coming? Dinner is almost finished.

Absolutely, give me a few minutes to hop in the shower, and I'm on my way.

She responded, I'm looking forward to seeing you. I'll leave the door unlocked. Let me know when you are in the house.

Ok cool...

I sit up on the couch, rub my face in my hands to clear my thoughts and gather myself. I pour another drink and finish off the glass. I go outside to puff the blunt a few more times and give one last thought to this situation. I mean, I did tell John I'll check on Apple, and I'm a man of my word. I put the blunt out, go back into the house and walk up the stairs to take a shower. As the time comes closer to seeing Apple, my anxiety for the situation starts to fade, and feelings of excitement begin to build. It's like the warm water washed the thick ash of guilt and anguish away for a new birth of contentment and happiness. At this point, my mind is made up. I'm not hesitating about this decision any longer. I'm all in. I get dressed, put on the baby powder and Cool Water cologne, you know the rest, get in my car and drive to John's house.

CHAPTER 6

When I got to John's house, John and Apple's cars were in the driveway, and the lights were on in the house. I get out of the car, walk up and open the door. From the front door, I can hear the shower going. I've been in their home several times but never upstairs to the main bathroom. I begin walking up the stairs towards the sound of the shower. As I walk down the hallway to the bathroom, I can smell the aroma of rosemary, vanilla and jasmine burning from the scented candles, and it fills the hallway. The bathroom door was cracked, so I pushed the door open. I can see Apple through the glass shower door. From the door, I can see her silhouette as she rubs the soapy towel across her breasts, thighs and ass. My heart starts to race, and my dick begins to stiffen like I'm a teenage boy anticipating his first piece of pussy. As I move closer to the moment I've been dreaming, fantasizing and waiting years to happen, no thoughts of April, John or my kids cross my mind. At this point, I knew I was in trouble, there's no turning back now, and I wasn't looking for the exit.

I call out to Apple to let her know I'm in the room; Apple, I'm here.

Apple shouts from the shower, Okay, Chris, make yourself comfortable in the den, and I'll be out shortly.

I walk back down the stairs into the den; I glance at John's desk in the corner of the room. I see a picture of us back when we were kids, another one at my graduation and another when he graduated from the academy. The den is immaculate, with rugged leather couches, rustic wooden coffee table, aged wine cabinet, beautifully crafted art pieces, the biggest television I've ever seen and a display of his medals earned in combat. Obviously, John has done some redecorating since the last time I've been here. I'm thinking, with all this beautiful, expensive shit, John should sell some of this shit to pay his bills. But that's neither here nor there right now. As I looked around the room, everything was in perfect order; this is expected from a military man. After about 15 minutes, I heard Apple come down the stairs, but she didn't come into the den. I followed the smell of food, and I found Apple in the kitchen. She's standing at the stove in a laced emerald green negligée, ass hanging from the bottom panties and her titties looking as if they were about to burst out the top. She's bent over into the oven and pulls out a pan. When she turns with the pan, she sees me standing in the kitchen doorway, and she says, I remember you said you like roast beef.

I catch myself starring at her perky titties and harden nipples, and I stumble out with, yeah, umm, I love roast beef. She says, good to hear, baby, go back in the den, relax, and I'll bring you a plate. After wiping the drool from my mouth, I agree and walk back to the den. A short time later, Apple comes in with a plate stacked with roast beef, carrots, potatoes and corn on the cob, truly my favorite meal. She lays the plate on the table in front of me and walks to the bar. It's beautiful to watch her walk; she has long, thick thighs, strongly defined calves, and she was wearing high heels, which made her firm ass cheeks bounce as she walked across the room. She gets to the bar and asks what I want to drink. You know I had to have the Dusse. She poured the drink, added a dash of Pepsi, again my favorite, came back over and sat next to me on the couch. She smelled amazing; the small beads of sweat from her pours after a hot shower oozed the sweet tone of a goddess as a crisp air of seduction filled the room. She picks up the fork from my plate, gathers a bit of roast and potatoes and places the fork up to my mouth to feed me the first bite. As she watches me chew, she asks, what do you think? Before I could answer, she fed me another bite slowly, then another. She takes out a napkin from under the plate and daps my lips. She moves closer to me and kisses me with the softest lips. After several kisses, she stands up and straddles my lap. She continues to kiss my lips and moves around to my ear, to my neck and to the top of my chest. I raise up to take my shirt off while she continues to kiss down my chest. My hands grip her ass, and her titties have exploded out her top. My dick is aching to burst out my pants as she reaches to unleash it. She gets to her knees, unzips my pants, pulls out my dick and places it in her mouth. She wraps her titties around the shaft while she keeps the head in her mouth. She gently moves her breasts up and down while sucking the head gently. I lay my head back against the couch and pray I don't bust too quick.

After several minutes, Apple raises to her feet and reaches for my hand. She takes hold of me and leads me to the bedroom. She places me on the bed and finishes removing my clothes. She walks over to the nightstand, picks up her phone, and music starts playing through the speakers. She reaches in the drawer, pulls out a fat sack of weed and begins to bust down a swisher. She finishes rolling the blunt, takes a deep puff and passes me the blunt. She stands to her feet; Summer Walker is playing in the background "Girls Need Love" as she begins to dance, move and subliminally dominate my mind space. Her ass starts clapping in celebration of this occasion, and with every snap of her ass cheeks, I see her pussy peeking at me through the bronze tint of the light from the window, inviting me to play, wanting me to stay, and needing me to heal years of sexual frustrations that have led us to this moment. She turns, looks back at me and asks, do you like that baby? I put my head back against the headboard, pull deeply of the weed, close my eyes and indulge fully in the moment. She walks over to the bed, takes off my pants and rolls me over. She sits on the small of my back and begins to massage my shoulders and work her way down my back. Her hands are both strong and gentle. She reaches for the candle, drips the hot wax on my back and kisses the places it hits, creating a beautiful mixture of pleasure and pain. Apple turns me onto my back, sits on top of me and slides my pulsating, rock-hard dick into her warm, tight pussy. As it slides in and out of her slowly, she moans deeply as to release all seeds of doubt into the atmosphere as a sacrifice to get out of the hell she's been trapped in with John. I pick her up off the bed and continue to pound into her against the wall. Over and over, deeper and deeper, harder and harder while she screams out in pleasure. Her pussy starts to cream as she holds me tighter, pulls me closer to her, and whispers in my ear. As the sweat trickles down my back, I no longer can hear the music as the strokes become more intense. I'm at home inside Apple, I'm safe, and I'm happy inside Apple. I throw her off me onto the bed to continue the mission. I bend her over; she moves into position with the perfect arch in her back; she looks back at me while I finish filling every hole in her body, physically and mentally. I wrap both hands around her neck and pull her head back. I continue thrusting my dick inside her violently and squeezing her throat tighter; the moment intensifies as I continue stroking, stroking and stroking, squeezing, pulling and choking. And then...all shit.

I hear and feel a snap in her neck, I release my hands

from Apple's neck, and her body falls limp and lifeless. I call out her name, I'm shaking her, and finally, I check for her pulse. I perform CPR, praying for a heartbeat. I continue breathing in her mouth and compressing her chest, nothing is beating, and nothing moves on her body.

Apple! Apple! I continue to scream her name in disbelief and panic. Please, Apple, get the fuck up. Please don't let this happen. What the fuck have I done? The room begins to spin, and the thought of me going to prison for murder fills my head, clouds my thoughts and impairs my judgment. I back up off the bed, sit in the chair and think about my next move. Should I call John? He knows I'm here, and he'll understand mistakes happen, right? Hell nah, I can't tell John I killed his wife. Maybe I should call the police; they'll understand a crime of passion. It was a mistake; I wasn't trying to kill her. Fuck! What should I do? I'll call my lawyer, tell him what happened and everything will be okay. Heart racing, jumping out of my chest, I picked up my phone to call the police, but I hesitated; I couldn't make the call.

I put my phone down and began picking up my clothes. After pulling my shirt over my head, I catch another glimpse of Apple lying on the bed. Even in death, she's beautiful. Tears begin to fall, my throat tightens, and an incredible sadness comes over me. I bend over the bed and pull her hair back to glance at her one last time. I can't believe this is happening. After sitting on the bed for a while, I pulled the blanket off the bed and managed to cover up her body. I straightened her hair, kissed her on the cheek and whispered in her ear, I'm sorry, Apple, please forgive me.

I gather the rest of my clothes and shoes and make my way out of the house. In my mind, I'm thinking I can't just leave her; it'll be a couple of days before John makes it home. She doesn't deserve that. So, I plan to hide the body or bury her where no one will find the body. Damn, that seems too harsh as well. My head is pounding, and I'm out of ideas. As I walk toward the front door, I smell smoke like something is burning. I rushed toward the kitchen to find flames and smoke filling the room. I cover my nose and mouth with a t-shirt; I grab the extinguisher and move toward the stove in an attempt to put out the flames. It was too late; the flames had reached a point I couldn't fight. I drop the extinguisher and run out the front door. I gather myself to look back at the house. I can see dark, thick smoke coming from the house. I'm about to get into my car when a thought comes to mind. This is a perfect opportunity to make it look like Apple was overcome by smoke and burned in the fire. I went back into the house; I picked up Apple's body off the bed to move her closer to the kitchen area so it'll look like she was trying to extinguish the fire. By this time, the flames were high, and the heat was tremendous; I could barely see through the thick smoke the fire had created. I got to the kitchen with Apple's body in my arms; flames were all around, burning my hands, which caused me to lose grip on her body. She falls from my arms, I'm unable to relocate her body, and I'm barely able to breathe. I'm able to get back to the front door; I ran out of the house and got back into my car. By this time, I can hear sirens in the distance. Apparently, someone has seen the smoke and called the fire department or the police. I pull out the driveway and head home. I passed the fire trucks, ambulance, and police cars on my way. I burst into tears, crushed by the anguish of what had just happened; it was an unbelievable ending that started as an incredible evening.

CHAPTER 7

I get home and pull into the driveway. It's about 4:30 am. My neighborhood is dead silent. No one is on the streets and there's no one to identify me coming home at this hour. Still tearful, I sit in the car for a while. I light a blunt from earlier and take a few pulls. I look down; my clothes are charred from the fire. I can smell the smoke; I'm sure the smell is circling through my car. After finishing the blunt, I went into the house. I got upstairs to take a shower. As I move the rag over certain areas of my body, I can feel sensitive spots from the flames and feel the burn spots on my arms and hands. After what seemed like hours, I get out of the shower and look through the drawers for ointment and bandages to cover the burns. The sun had risen by this time as I walked out into the bedroom. I closed the curtains and lay across the bed.

I cannot believe this shit. How did this happen? How am I going to face John? How am I going to tell April? Even if everyone believes my story, how will I face myself? Apple didn't deserve this fate. I don't deserve this fate. Now I'm facing a life-changing situation. And for what? One night of pleasure? How could I be so selfish? So many questions fill my head with no answers to any. Still, in my robe with my arm and hands covered in bandages, a sorrowful cry begins while I continue to think about last night. It's like it's not real. I wish I could awake from this nightmare. After I get my mind together, I get in bed and finally fall asleep.

I awake later in the day to a million texts, several from April and hundreds from John. I scroll through a few, and each one from John gets more aggressive and desperate.

John texts, what's going on? I'm getting calls about a fire...

Another text, pick up the fucking phone, what the fuck is going on... Another one, Chris, call me as soon as you get this...

April texts, where are you? John has been calling me about a fire at his house or something...

Missed call after missed call, my anxiety increases. I can't go missing. It'll be strange for me not to answer the calls. My head is spinning. What's my next play? Unfortunately, I decided to leave Apple in the fire; therefore, I must keep this story. I don't want to go to jail, I don't want to lie to John, and I don't want my wife to find out about any of this stuff. I take a deep breath to gather myself. I call April first to gauge John's level of understanding of the situation.

April answers, Chris, what's going on? Where are you? John has been calling all morning. What is he saying?

He's saying he's getting calls from his neighbors. They're saying there was a fire at this house, and he can't contact Apple. I've tried calling Apple as well; she's not answering. Have you heard from her?

No, I haven't heard anything. I have missed calls and texts from John but nothing from Apple. I'm at the house, let me call John and find out what's going on.

Ok, call me back as soon as you find out anything. I will.

As soon as I hang up the phone with April, John calls. I stare at the phone for a few rings and answer the phone hesitantly.

Hello.

John tearful, Chris, what the fuck is going on? Have you heard from Apple? Neighbors told me my house burned down; no one had seen or heard from Apple. She is not answering the phone, and she's not texting me back. I'm going crazy, Chris.

No, I haven't heard from Apple since last night. I spoke to her briefly last night, but nothing since then.

Where in the fuck could she be? How the fuck did the house catch fire? I canceled my surgery, and I'm headed home. I'm about to get on the plane now. I'll be there in about an hour. Can you pick me up from the airport?

Yeah, no problem. Call me when you touch down. In the meantime, I'll drive past your house and see if I can find out any information or maybe find Apple.

Tearful and anxious John finished, please Chris, I'm going crazy here, find out something, and I'll call as soon as I arrive.

Don't worry. I got you.

I can't believe I just lied to John about Apple and his house. On top of that, I have to pick him up from the airport and live this nightmare all over again. After a few minutes of staring at the wall, I got up, got dressed and left the house, headed to John's house. All types of shit continue to cloud my mind. The what-ifs and why not's race through my thoughts. The unbelievable and the unthinkable happened at the same time. I arrive at John's house, in the light of the day; I can't believe the destruction the fire caused. The house completely burned to the ground. There were no structural columns, no trees in the yard, and Apple's car even burned. It was like nothing was ever there; only the foundation remained. I know it's sick; on the inside, I'm a bit relieved. I just may be able to get out of this situation without anyone knowing what I've done, what I did to Apple, what I've done to my friendship with John and my marriage to April. I walk closer to the house to get a closer look. Nothing is recognizable; if you didn't know a beautiful home stood here before, nothing would clue you in. Looking at the rumble and water-soaked remains of the house, I openly chuckle a bit. I'm going to get away with this if I can keep my shit together. While standing in what was the driveway, April texts me.

We are on the road headed home. We should be there in about 3-4 hours. Ok, be careful, and I'll see you all soon.

Have you spoken to John?

Yes, he's on an airplane, and he should be here soon. Have you heard from Apple?

No, I haven't heard anything. That's not like her not to respond to my texts or phone calls. I'm getting worried.

Yeah, me too. I'm at John's house; you wouldn't believe the damage. It's crazy out here. Let me know if you hear anything else.

Ok. I'm going to pick John up from the airport, and I'll see y'all later tonight.

While sitting in my car, I roll a blunt, puff it and smile again. Although regret is a familiar foe, at this time, I feel good courting happiness because I can see a way out of this trouble. It's selfish, I know, but self-preservation is at the forefront of my mind. After about 20 minutes, my phone rings, it's John, he's at the airport. I catch out on the highway en route to the airport. I pull around to the passenger pick-up area. I see John at the curb, waving his hands to get my attention. He gets in the car, crying uncontrollably; his anxiety is on ten.

Take me to the house, Chris, please.

No other words were spoken. I didn't know what to say. I had no words. I can feel his anxiety growing as he smokes cigarette after cigarette. It was a twenty-minute drive to his house; he smoked about 20 cigarettes, crying and mumbling something I didn't understand; I knew he wasn't talking to me, so I stayed silent the whole ride. When we get to the house or what's left of the house, John jumps out of the car before the car stops completely. I put the car in park and watch as he walks up to what he once called home. He rambles through the rumble, falls to his knees and bursts into a screeching yell.

Seeing him cry profusely quickly brought me back to regret. At that moment, I wanted to break down and confess everything about that night. I couldn't bring myself to do it. I just sat there. I wanted to console my friend with all the answers to questions he's praying to God to answer; I just sat there, not saying one word. I walked up to the house and walked over to where he was standing. He continues to look around what is left of his home. He began reminiscing about the life he had in his home. He walks to the back of what would've been the bedroom. I see him rambling through some items and putting things in his pockets and a shoulder bag. After he finishes gathering the items, he comes back toward the front of the house.

Do you want me to take you to the police station? Maybe they can give you answers to what caused the fire.

John's response was odd; I paid it no mind at the time. He said I hadn't heard from Apple. It's not like her to disappear like this. I know something bad has happened to her. She's a strong woman, a good person; I pray she's not suffering, I pray she's okay and returns to me. Hey, do you remember when Apple transferred to our school? Laughing and smiling, he continued, she was so skinny with that big ole head and those fire red Jordan 5's. In my eyes, she was the most beautiful girl I'd ever seen. I was so nervous to talk to her.

I know, I had to talk to her for you. I have never seen you nervous around girls. I knew she had to be special to have you tripping over her.

Yeah, she was special. When the new girl came to a school, it was open season on who would get her first, so I played it cool.

Nah nigga, you were scared.

Whatever, I played it cool. I watched her turn down dude after dude, from the most popular guys, the smartest guys, even the entire basketball team. Still smiling with a proud sense of accomplishment on his face, he continued, she was loyal. Never did I hear about her being too friendly to other guys. Never did I think she was unfaithful to me. Never did I imagine living without her. I'm not a spiritual person; I know God is punishing me.

Why you say that?

Because of the choices I've made and the choices I influenced for my selfish reasons. He turns and looks me in the eyes; I'm sorry, Chris. I'm sorry for asking you to do something against the love for your wife, your family and your beliefs.

Listen, you didn't ask me to do anything I didn't want to do. Knowing the truth about Apple's death, this was probably the moment I should've told him about what happened last night. April was right about me. I am a coward. I only cared about myself because I could not bring myself to tell him the truth. Even after seeing my brother crying, pleading and begging for answers, I couldn't give it to him.

We pull up to the police station. John gets out of the car. I roll the window down; John bends over and looks through the open window.

Thanks for bringing me.

Do you want me to come in with you?

Nah, I'm good. I'll call you later if I have any problems.

Ok, cool, make sure you call me as soon as you hear anything.

He taps the car and walks into the police station. Nervous as fuck, I light a blunt and drive home. What the fuck have I done?

CHAPTER 8

I haven't heard from John since I dropped him off at the police station, nor have I heard about Apple's disappearance from any authorities. Although I'm getting a little nervous, it seems as if I've avoided murder charges. If John finds out what happened in his house before it burned, I know I'm fucked and moreover, I probably deserve it. My wife and kids were in the den while I sat alone in the basement with my favorite drink, Dusse, straight. As I began to realize the magnitude of my decisions over the past few days, I begin to become disgusted with myself. Fucking my best friend's wife was terrible; murdering his wife was unthinkable, and lying about it is unforgivable. For what? For money? For lust? I don't know truly; as usual, the answer is somewhere between. I could have easily given him the money for the surgery and avoided all this, but I didn't, and it's fucking with me.

On top of that, I love my wife, my family, I would never want this to come to light. So, what am I to do? The truth is the sex was amazing. It made me realize what I was missing with April and what I miss about being treated like a king. Apple brought out feelings I hadn't felt in a while. I still can't believe this happened to Apple. Shit, I can't believe this happened to me. At times, the feeling of guilt and sorrow overwhelms me. At other times, I'm daydreaming, fantasizing about that pussy with every free moment that passes. I know, I'm a sick individual. April doesn't deserve the monster I've become, furthermore, I don't like the monster I've become. Lusting and craving for Apple, not being emotionally available for April's needs is a cross I never wanted to carry in my marriage. But here I am, tangled in a web of lies and deceit and, even worst, death. There is one thing for sure, April and I will have to talk about this and clear the air. I want to tell her about John's proposal and the night with Apple so we can move on and hopefully get past this situation. As I take another sip of my drink, I pray for the courage to tell the truth about what I've done. Unfortunately, nothing yet.

Later that night, I called John to invite him over for dinner. He didn't answer the phone. I called several times and left several messages with no response. The last time we spoke, he seemed okay, but it's hard to know if he'll be okay with this weighing on him. I lay back in my chair, light a blunt, turn on the game and continue sipping on my drink. Shortly after, I hear a knock on the door. I must have dozed off because it scared the shit out of me. The room was smoky, and for a moment, I flashed back to seeing Apple collapsed in the burning kitchen. I quickly gather myself and my son comes into the room. He asked if I'd seen his game for the PS5. I reached down by the chair and handed him the disc.

Dad, why is the room full of smoke and what's that smell?

I usually don't smoke in the house, never when my kids are home, but tonight was different. Son, don't worry about the smoke; everything is okay. Where's mom and your sister?"

They are upstairs asleep. What happened to dinner?

We ate dinner about an hour ago; mom saved you a

plate; I think it's in the oven. Damn, why didn't anyone come to tell me dinner was ready?

I don't know. Can I go over to my friend's house and play video games? What time is it?

It's 7 0'clock, dad. Dennis's mother said it was okay.

His friend lived next door; I agreed to let him go. He leaves the room excited. Tell your mother you're leaving.

Through all the weed smoke and liquor, I'm still having this feeling of guilt. It continues to build, filling my soul. I haven't slept well since the incident, I have to face the issue, and it's inevitable, I need to talk to someone about what happened to Apple. I need a conversation with John. I've deceived the two people I go to for counsel. I'm on my own with this situation. Only I can make this right. Right about that time, my phone rings...it's John. I rush to answer the phone; Hello.

What's up? I missed your call; what's going on? John starts.

Nothing really. I haven't heard from you. I was checking on you. I was going to invite you over for dinner; apparently, the family ate without me. How are you doing?

Oh, okay, I appreciate the thought, but I'm not hungry. Listen, I wanted to know if we could talk?

The tone of his voice was uneasy and calm. Nervously, I said, yeah, of course, what's up? Chris, you know I don't like talking over the phone.

Okay, come by the house. I'll send a car for you.

No thanks, I'll take an Uber. I'm on my way as soon as the car pulls up.

After hanging up, I began to think, what the hell does he want to discuss that he can't talk about over the phone? My thoughts started racing in multiple directions, but they all ended in sadness when I began to think about the times he cried to me about the depth of the love he had for Apple and the fact he would never betray her in any way. I started thinking of my commitment and the vows I made to April. The guilty sank deeper. I hit the blunt, praying these thoughts would go away. Unfortunately, the blunt was not enough to calm my nerves; the pain was enormous.

John gets to the house. He calls me saying he's outside. When I looked out the window, I saw he was wearing a black suit and carrying a black tote bag. I walk to the door and let him in the house through the garage. From the moment he walked into the room, the tension was thick as fuck. It was obvious he was there for business. I tried to lighten the moment, I offered him a beer; he declined. John never declines a cold one; this visit isn't the friendly type.

Still nervous and with an awkward smile, I ask, what's going on, brother? Everything good? Brother huh? Are we brothers?

Yeah, what you mean, we always have been.

John starring intensely, if we are brothers, shouldn't brothers tell each other the truth? Brothers don't harm each other. Brothers have each other's back. A brother would not have done what you've done.

I instantly teared up, and my nervousness instantly turned back to regret. I never wanted to hurt him this way. I should've just given him the money for the procedure and ignored my childish lusts. My selfishness has led us to this place. I just stood there, no answers, no excuses and no way out of this situation.

John continued, you, of all people, know what she meant to me. And you took advantage of the situation. I told you everything about my struggles, and everything went out the window when you heard the opportunity to fuck my wife, Brother!

All I can say is I'm sorry, John. I never meant for things to be this way. When we talked about this, you told me you were okay with this, and you wanted it to be me instead of someone you don't know, remember?

It's too late for sorry, bruh. And you're right; I was okay with the plan. I would've agreed to anything to make Apple happy. What I didn't agree to was you murdering Apple and leaving her to die! Now, I have a new plan. You're going to pay for your disrespect.

John, it was a mistake, I didn't want things to go that way. You have to believe me. I wouldn't do anything to hurt you or Apple.

Fuck that Chris, you lied to me! You said you had no idea what happened to Apple. Come to find out, you know exactly what happened to Apple. You fucking killed Apple, Chris!

Disgusted by his tone, I replied, I didn't murder Apple, it was an accident. Excuse me John but let's not get it too twisted; you came to me with this shit, and Apple had no problem with it. You're talking like I planned for this to happen.

Is that how you feel, my brother? John asked with an intense look on his face. You think just because you say it's a mistake, you're not gonna pay for what you've done?

John, what do you me to do? What happened can't be undone. I can't bring Apple back. I'm so sorry this happened to all of us.

Once again, Chris. You wanna cry like you're the victim. Apple is dead and you stand there alive, with your family like everything is okay. No brother, everything is not okay and trust me your gonna for this shit.

Feeling the heightened mood, I attempted to allow calmer minds to prevail. John, let's be calm before we say things we don't mean. Unfortunately, there was no way to calm him down.

I'm saying exactly what I mean.

I yelled out with an aggressive tone, well, fuck the extra talk and get to what you want to say! Aight cool, here it is. I had a camera in the room for surveillance.

Confused, what the fuck? You recorded your wife and me fucking? Why would you want to see that?

John looked at me angrily, No, nigga, I didn't want to

see you fucking my wife. I have cameras throughout the house for security purposes. I wanted to see the footage because they told me they found Apple in the house when I went to the police station. The police couldn't conclude what had happened. Her body was burned so severely, the medical examiner couldn't declare a cause of death. They are going to declare her death as accidental but they couldn't quite conclude one other detail. Do you know what that one thing is? Can you guess where they found her, Chris? I bet you already know because it was you who put her there. And you know what the kicker is, Chris? Not only was she burned in the kitchen, but the autopsy discovered her neck was broken. How could this happen? For the police, it was simple. She attempted to put the fire out, fell to the floor and somehow her neck was broken. Seems like a reasonable conclusion. But I had to know what happened for sure. How did Apple break her neck and burn in a fire? Then, that's when I remembered the surveillance cameras were linked to my phone. I was able to recover the footage of that night. To answer your question, yes, I watched it, over, over, over and over again. I wanted to try and figure out every scenario in which this could happen. After I watched the first time, I wanted to know why you would leave Apple there to burn in the fire whether she was already dead or not. But I couldn't figure it out. I watched it a second and a third time. Still, I couldn't come up with any ideas that would satisfy me. Not only did you fuck my wife, but you also snapped her neck, left, came back, left her there to burn, you sick, selfish muthafucka. You could've called for help. You saved yourself and left my Apple there to die alone. The thing is, on the recording, it's obvious you didn't murder her. Let's call it a crime of passion. But, there's no need to recall all the details, you were there, and you know the rest. Although you would have been charged with manslaughter, you're a bitch ass rich boy with a golden reputation in the community; it's possible nothing much would have happened to you. When I was in Nashville on the phone with you, I asked you if you knew anything about what happened to Apple. You said nothing. After you picked me up from the airport, you said nothing. You could have told me because I was your brother, and you decided to say nothing. You thought you had the perfect setup to get off and not be held responsible for this situation, right? You watched me cry until my eyes were sore, wondering what happened to my wife; you said nothing. Therefore, at this point, I want you to say nothing. Lucky for you, I will not inform the police of this footage. The what, why and how are no longer important. The only important thing is how your wife would feel knowing you fucked Apple, watched her burn, and how much money you would pay to keep her and the police from knowing what you've done.

My head started spinning. The thought of April knowing would destroy my family. My selfish act has brought me to this place. A place I never wanted to be, and I'm the only one to blame for this outcome. Therefore, the choice is easy. I will have to pay for this one way or the other; my money or life.

Why would you do this to me? Why would you hurt my family with this bullshit?

Bullshit? You chose to do this. You've always wanted to fuck my wife. What, you think I didn't know? Now you stand there, calling me brother and questioning why I would do this to you. Nigga, you did this to yourself a long time ago.

Okay, John, how much will it take to make this, and you, disappear? Laughing, oh, you really thought this is about money, my nigga?

What the fuck else is there, John?

Do you remember the talk we had on my wedding day?
Yeah of course.

And I told you I would die for this woman? Nigga, stop
with the riddles. What are you saying?

John reaches in his pocket; I'm saying I'll kill for her
as well.

John pulls out a blade from his pocket. I want you
dead. There's no way you will walk this earth with the
satisfaction of fucking my wife, killing her and living.
So, you are in the same situation you put my wife in,
fucked.

What? Panicking, I struggle to find words to buy time
and talk him down, but it's too late. The look on his
face is one I've never seen before, and he looks as if
there's no more talking to be done. John has been
trained through the military to kill. I knew I had little
chance of stopping him. My wife and daughter are in
the bedroom asleep, and this stupid muthafucker is in
my face threatening to murder me in my house. The
thoughts in my mind continue to race. Then, the door
opens.

Not expecting the door to open, John turns and sticks
the knife in the stomach of my wife. I guess she heard

the screaming and came into the room. As she began to bleed out, I rushed toward John, knocking him and April onto the floor. I began swinging and punching him in the face.

I look over toward April, and she is crawling toward the kitchen. Before I can focus back on John, he stabs me in the side several times. He pushes me off of him. I turn over on my back, looking toward the ceiling, and all I can think of is my family and me dying on the floor. John gets on top of me and sits on my stomach, making it harder to breathe. Blood begins coming out my mouth. I heard April gasping for air, trying to reach the phone. John must have heard her as well. He looks me in the eyes, smiles and stabs me in the chest. He gets off me and walks toward April, crawling to the kitchen. He drags April by her hair back into the room with me. As she pleads for her life, I can only lay there helpless, choking on my blood and unable to move. People talk of their lives flashing before them before death; mine didn't flash; I only saw darkness.

John asks April, do you know why I'm doing this to you?

She screams out, No! Why John? Why are you doing this to us? He looks at me and asks, should I tell her or you?

April continues to cry and bleed onto the floor. My eyes fill with tears and my heart with regret. I vowed never to allow harm to my family. At this moment, I finally understood what being a husband and father should've meant to me.

As John awaits my decision, he screams out, Tell her or I will.

Even in this dying moment, I didn't have the courage to tell her the truth about me. After becoming frustrated with my hesitance, he tells her the story as he holds the knife to her neck. He tells April about the proposal and the night that ensued. How I fucked his wife for the money they needed for the surgery, the thirst I held for Apple, the resentment he felt toward me in his heart and the murder of the one person he held dearest. He continued to tell her, in detail, about that night.

April's face turned toward me with disgust. She didn't say a word; her look said it all. How could you do this to your family? How could you allow this to happen to us? I had no answers to any of the questions.

After he told her about how I fucked Apple and the feeling of betrayal he felt, he looked at me and cut her throat, ear to ear. He looked over at me and said, I'm not done. Where's your little princess? He walked to the back of the house, where my daughter was asleep. Blood and tears ran from my eyes, and all I could do was lay there, helpless and afraid. I began blacking out, going in and out of consciousness. I don't know how long I was out, when I open my eyes, I can see my wife on the floor beside me, dead. I hear John coming and the voice of my daughter screaming. He dragged her into the room with us. She continued to scream. I tried to speak; I couldn't; all I could do was cry and bleed. He puts her where I can see her face, pulls out a 9 mm and shoots my daughter in the head. Her blood sprays out on me as I continue to bleed out on the floor. He comes back over towards me, pulls out the blade and stabs me again in the side of my head.

Whispering, he says, fuck you, fuck you and everything you love, brother. You took Apple away from me, so I'm taking everything from you. John rolls off me and sits up in the corner. He pulls out the gun from his hip, places the gun on the bottom of his neck. As I lie there, completely unable to move, I can hear John attempt to explain his actions.

Chris, our friendship meant the world to me, but

Apple, Apple was my world. I understand it was unfair for what I asked of you. I felt I had no choice. I was selfish in my decision to ask you to help save my marriage in that way. It wasn't about the money. I want you to know I didn't serve you my wife for the money. She was about to leave me, and I couldn't bear the thought. I thought I could handle the consequences, maybe I could, but the way you attempted to cover up her death was unforgivable. Why didn't you just tell me what happened? Why didn't you pull her out of the house when the fire started? I guess it doesn't matter now. Although it doesn't mean shit, I am sorry for all this bullshit. I wish I could take it all back, but we can never go back. You made your decision, and I've made mine. Unfortunately, we were both wrong.

John cocks the pistol, places the gun under his neck and...

Most people believe the greatest trick the devil performs is making people believe he exists. For me, the devil's real trick is giving you everything you've dreamed of and watching you fuck it up. Watching you destroy everything and everyone around you while he laughs at you promising yourself you'll never do that bullshit again. He laughs will you pray to God; If I only had that one other thing, I can be better and I could be better than I was yesterday. If I had the opportunity, if I looked like that person or if I born another race, I could show them what I could really do. You see the trick is you knowing all the while its a lie but you still pretend to be what society calls normal because you're scared to be you. You're scared because, what if they really know how felt about them, what you truly believed in and how far you are willing to go to be who you are. Would they still love you? Living a lie is like living New Year's Eve over and over again. There's a constant countdown to your life; there's only a short amount of time to be you. My advice to being you is to never look to man for answers because he'll always bite the apple.

3...2...1 Happy New Year, good luck mutherfucker; you're gonna need it!!!

About the Author

CHRISTOPHER PEOPLES was born in Chicago, Illinois and raised in Meridian, Mississippi. Given this unique view of life growing up, Chris was fascinated with human interactions amongst men and women, rich and poor, Black and White people. Through this lens, Chris examines the choices people make to survive in their own mind, body and spirit. These ideals led Chris to study Psychology at the University of Southern Mississippi where he developed a thesis about duality personalities. A theory where a person can be both saint and sinner, angel and demon, good and evil interchangeably based on what is needed at different times. In Chris's debut as an author, Bitten Apple explores the issue of how a man's desire for a forbidden fruit leads to chaos and destruction.

Made in the USA
Columbia, SC
09 June 2024

36395779R00061